FRAT BOY FUN

Erotic Stories From The Dungeon

Book 3

BJ Cuffs

Table of Contents

<u>Chapter One</u>
Esmerelda

A layer of grime and dirt caked the walls of the frat house, and my stomach churned just looking at it. It was a job that paid well. I was very good at cleaning up other people's messes. My people were trained meticulously to turn the other cheek, but there were rare exceptions.

The things I had seen in this house were things I could never close my eyes to. It was burned into my memory. The furnace of body odor that blasted me in the face as I entered one of the bedrooms was enough to make any self-respecting woman walk the other way.

The dirty jockstrap lying on the floor had a pungent scent of masculinity burned inside. A team jersey hung in disarray over the dresser's edge, and the bedsheets were rumpled and well worn. Pulling back the sheets, I found a used condom crusted to the under layer.

I had a feeling my staff was in for a rude awakening. They were paid to provide a detailed service. I wasn't asking any of them to do anything that I wouldn't do myself. There was a lengthy list of demands from the frat boys. They wanted us to be their mothers without the shame of being called out for their actions.

"I apologize on behalf of my brothers. This is disgraceful, and I will bring up the manner of hygiene at our next meeting. Some of them are still living like they're in their parent's basement. I can assure you, not every room is like this one," Hunter stated over my shoulder, breathing down the back of my neck.

"It's not anything I haven't seen before." I lied through my teeth.

"I wish I could get it through their thick skulls. There's a time to party and a time to study. There are a few that can't make that distinction. I don't know what it's gonna take. I'm at my wit's end trying to figure it out."

Hunter was the one paying us. He had a perfect smile, with dark hair that waved down to his shoulders. He dressed impeccably without a single hair out of place. He knew how to present himself to a lady. It was nice to see some hometown values could be retained even in the big city.

The black drapes in the room hid the garbage of takeout boxes and fast food containers littering the floor. There was a buzz of flies surrounding the leftover food. It wasn't the first time I had seen something like that, but it usually involved shut-ins or abandoned houses.

It's disgusting. This is no way to live.

"I think we both know they're never going to change without a good reason. You can't be responsible for their actions. It's not fair to place the blame squarely at your feet. I commend you for making allowances for them. I don't think that I could be so forgiving," I said, using a ski pole to pick up dirty underwear, tossing them into the unused hamper in the corner.

"You deserve a bonus for going above and beyond the call of duty. Unfortunately, we have to adhere to a budget. It doesn't include an added incentive. I will have a word with them. I don't know what good it's going to do, but something has to be done," he said, exasperated.

I listened as his footsteps disappeared down the hallway.

It took almost an hour to finish one room. The bathroom had me attempting to hold my breath while I scrubbed the toilet. The soap scum in the shower took an industrial-strength cleaner usually reserved for toxic environments. By the time I was done, though, you could barely tell it hadn't always been pristine.

The glass sink was spotless, and the hair in the drain pulled free.

Every inch of the white tile was sparkling.

It stood to reason the place wouldn't remain clean for long under those adverse conditions, but if it did, I might be out of a job.

I went down to the kitchen, grabbed a cold bottle of water, and placed it against my chest. There was a discussion going on in the dining room. I adjusted what most people in my inner circle of friends considered a disability. It wasn't a handicap. I didn't need the hearing aid, but it came in handy.

"She was fucking tight, and I almost lost it the moment I stuck it in her. It took a little bit of convincing, but she finally let me fuck her in the ass. It felt like a hot dog down a hallway. It wasn't her first time. I imagine there was a train of guys before me. What A fucking slut," the guy bellowed, a chorus of laughter following his words.

"Brock, you know how to pick 'em', but maybe next time you can leave us sloppy seconds. When she took that walk of shame, it was more like running from her bad decisions. At least she left something for you to remember her by. These are still wet. I think you both know what I'm going to do with them." Chet dangled the blue lace panties in the air.

I could see the two of them around the huge mahogany table. Chet was holding the piece of fabric to his nose.

From the shreds of what was left, I could tell Brock definitely had a thing for liking it rough.

"Dude, I don't care what you do with them. I've already had my fun. Just don't return them to me," he insisted, his face twisted in disgust. Chet swung the panties into the air and then smiled knowingly

"I know…I know...they are a little ripped. What can I say? We both had a rough night, if you know what I mean," Brock replied with a chuckle, flexing his big ham hocks in the air to show his bruteness and sculpted physique.

I snuck back upstairs and into his room, where I had spent over an hour tidying up. My business card found its way onto his black night table next to the blinking green light of his alarm clock. There was a handwritten note on the back.

"Anything goes…".

It's time to take off the kid gloves.

***

Brock

Next to studying, the worst thing about going away to college was having to clean up after yourself. Up until the day I left for school, my mother did everything for me around the house. I always had clean clothes, came home to fresh sheets on my bed, and had a home-cooked meal every night. She'd been a stay-at-home mom ever since she became pregnant with me and treated housework as her job.

Which is what any good woman should do.

Thankfully, Hunter got us a group rate for laundry service. All of the guys in our fraternity house loaded up some garbage bags and handed them over to the company. He also struck a deal with a local cleaning service, which I thought came with putting my clean clothes away. Imagine my surprise when I came home from classes one day and found all of them on my freshly made bed.

Would it have killed the bitch to put them away for me?

After the cleaning service left, I headed back upstairs to get some studying done. Chet went into his adjacent bedroom, where I could overhear him jerking off for a good half an hour. No doubt with the used, dirty, ripped panties from the girl I fucked last night.

My cock got hard just thinking about it again.

I couldn't remember her name, but getting into those panties hadn't been too much work. Just one thrust into her pussy, and I almost came, though. She was so tight, in fact, I was convinced she was a virgin.

Which is why I assumed her ass was even tighter. Sadly, I probably could have shoved my fist inside. If I had to guess, she encouraged guys to fuck her ass so her future husband would think she was a virgin.

At least I got to cum on her face, though.

I plopped down on my freshly-made bed and reached over to my nightstand, right as I heard Chet getting ready to cum.

"Oh fuck!"

"Bust a nut in her panties, bro!" I yelled across the hallway. A handful of my fraternity brothers burst out laughing.

While opening my nightstand drawer, a business card fell onto the ground:

The Dungeons ~ Anything Goes ~ Mistress Esmerelda

Below the business name was an address, which I quickly searched online. All I found was a local business that dealt with restaurant furnishings. It didn't take me long to figure out that within the basement of that business was an underground sex club.

Who the fuck is Mistress Esmerelda?

I realized that it must have fallen out of that girl's purse and that she moonlighted there for extra cash. The thought of fucking her hallway of an asshole again didn't turn me on, but surely a sex dungeon had other women working there. Hell, the girl's boss was probably Mistress Esmerelda and carried business cards with her.

Our fraternity calendar showed we had nothing going on that night, so on a whim, I called the number…and instantly got hard at the seductive voice on the other end of the phone.

"The Dungeons, who's calling?"

"Um, hi. Sorry, but who's Mistress Esmerelda?"

"Mistress Esmerelda? She's one of our most popular dominatrix's. Are you a new client?" *No way was the chick last night a Dominatrix.* "Sir?"

"Yes, I guess I am."

"She has an opening tonight at nine o'clock. Would you like to meet with her?"

I had heard about Female Domination before and was under the impression that they still submitted to men with big cocks. It had something to do with Alpha versus beta males, and at eleven inches, I was definitely an Alpha.

"Yes, I would love to meet with her."

By the time I was done scheduling my appointment, I had come up with several scenarios in which I would get Mistress Esmerelda-whoever she was-to submit to me. Even if she wasn't a Dominatrix who submitted to Alpha cocks, then I'd still find a way into her panties. After all, I was one of the hottest guys on campus, and no woman had ever turned me down.

Who the fuck do these feminists think they are, anyway?

***

Esmerelda

"Yeah, Brock will be in when we open," the Dungeon owner, Celeste said, yawning. "Apparently, he found your card but said he wasn't sure where it came from."

I chuckled. "Oh my, how peculiar."

"Mhmm," Celeste replied. "Hey, I have nothing against marketing, that's for sure."

Brock had taken the bait and was about to find out what his most profound and darkest desires were and all at the hands of a very hungry dominatrix.

I had the spot in the deepest part of the Dungeon basement where nobody would be able to hear him scream in terrified delight.

The pure intoxicating black leather catsuit adorned my body from head to toe, including the mask. It wasn't likely he would recognize me with my crimson lipstick and makeup, but I wasn't taking any chances. The last thing I wanted was to have a reputation that would precede me. It was better to remain anonymous, away from the prying eyes of others.

I was ready for him, sitting in my perfected space, my lips pursed, staring around the room. I liked to get there early, readying myself for the evening's events—the types of nights I had needed to be planned out. Surprises weren't fun when you were working as one of the more hardcore Dominatrix's in the building.

A knock signified Brock's imminent arrival.

He took a step back the second the door opened, suddenly quite nervous about what he'd gotten himself into. My tongue grazed my top lip as I waited for him to cross the threshold, slamming the door shut once he was inside.

"Good evening, Brock. Welcome to the Dungeons."

Chapter Two
Esmerelda

The smirk on Brock's face grew wider as he looked me up and down, wondering who the woman was behind the mask.

"Who are you, exactly?"

"I'm Mistress Esmerelda, Brock. Didn't you book an appointment with me this evening?"

He casually formed a loud, obnoxious green bubble with his chewing gum while nodding with approval.

"Well yeah, but…"

"But what, Brock? Were you expecting a twenty-one-year-old drunk sorority slut? Or is that just something you do at your fraternity house?"

His blue eyes glazed over as he took a step back, suddenly regretting his decision.

"Look, maybe I'm in the wrong place. It's just that I found this business card on my nightstand, and I don't know how it got there, but suddenly I'm getting the wrong vibe." He nervously looked over my shoulder, eyeing my black steel table with a plush, cherry-red mattress. "Did she say anything about me?"

Now we were getting somewhere.

"What girl are you referring to, Brock?"

He ran his hand through his dirty-blonde, tousled hair.

"Um, you know. That girl from last night."

I took a step closer to him, my heels clicking along the floor and bouncing off the dungeon walls.

"You don't even know her name, do you Brock? In fact, you probably don't know the names of any of the girls you fuck."

A trickle of sweat ran down his face, causing his tinted moisturizer to leave a streak as water droplets fell onto his dark polo shirt. Brock dabbed at the sweat with his cream-colored sweater draped loosely around his muscular shoulders.

By all outward appearances, he was the quintessential, self-entitled frat boy who didn't understand the word 'no.' Not that I would place him in the bin with sociopaths who forced themselves upon women, though. But not only was he not put-off with the concept of female domination, he actually seemed intrigued.

He slowly stepped back into my room with his obnoxiously bright white sneakers.

"Look, I just came here to have a good time. But I'm new to this female domination shit, so go easy on me, okay?"

Brock walked into my chamber and looked around, eyeing all of my bondage equipment. I caught a glimpse of his arm muscles as he ran his fingers on a black gate.

"We won't be using that room tonight, Brock."

The outline of a decent-sized cock formed within his khakis as he stood in front of the red bed, suddenly seeming very eager to start our session.

"So, what will we be using tonight?" I pointed my fingers towards an eight-inch dildo sitting upon a shelf. "Are you out of your fucking mind, woman? Look, at most, I thought I'd get a spanking!"

I cracked my whip against the floor, breaking him from his shock.

"First of all, if you want a good, hard spanking, then you'll earn it by calling me, Mistress Esmerelda. Second of all, are you suggesting that you've never even considered anal sex?"

"Hey, I love fucking a-wait a minute, is that why she sent me here? Because she thought I'd want to get ass-fucked?"

"Why on earth would she think that, Brock? Was the sorority slut you fucked last night into anal sex?"

The smirk on his face grew by several inches.

"Let's just say it wasn't her first time."

Brock stood still as I circled him, keeping his hands deep in his pockets. Guys like him were a bit harder to break into. My leather-clad breasts pushed into his back.

"Take off your shirt for me, Brock."

He eagerly removed his shirt, hitting me with a whiff of his cologne. Brock had an excellent upper-body. My whip ran over his six-pack abs, tracing the outline as he seemed quite proud of his gym accomplishments.

"I gotta look good for the ladies, Mistress Esmerelda."

"Now, take off the rest of your clothing."

Brock began to quickly strip until he, and his cock, were standing at a full salute. It was impressive at over 9 inches and thick enough to choke a horse. My cunt ached for a brief second.

My upper-lip snarled upon seeing his black ankle socks still covering his feet.

"What words didn't you understand? Nothing is going to happen while you're wearing those."

"What difference does it make if I'm wearing socks? Besides, I'm going to need leverage to fuck that sweet ass of yours after you're done licking mine."

The crack of the whip against his chest made him wince in pain.

"Oh, I'm sorry. Do you not like pain? Tell me, *Brock*, do you consider that when a girl tells you that anal is too painful?"

He didn't answer me, though. Instead, I watched with amusement as he quickly ripped off his socks.

God...he is sexy. I can't wait to get my hands on him. The way he looks frightened...I want a taste. No. I have to be patient.

"I'm afraid you have the wrong idea. Anal lubrication, not my tongue, is the only thing going into your asshole. Well, that and this."

Brock's lower-lip quivered in fear as I brought down Elvis, pressing the tip of the disturbingly life-like dildo to my crimson lips.

"I didn't come here for that, Mistress Esmerelda. I'm not going to say that I haven't been curious. Maybe we could start small, like have you finger my ass after lubing it up."

"I don't do small, Brock. You know, for such a so-called Alpha male, you sure are coming off as a whiny little bitch right now. The door is right there, you know.'

Brock started out through the door, which was still wide open.

"Why haven't you shut it yet, Mistress Esmerelda?"

"Relax," I said while pointing to the red mattress. "Since you haven't gotten dressed and run out the door yet, I'll take that as permission to proceed. Now, lay face down on the mattress."

Brock's tall, six-foot-body walked over to the mattress and carefully laid down.

"Please don't hurt me, Mistress Esmerelda. I know that I treat women horribly, but please don't go too far."

As I fastened Brock's hands and ankles to shackles, I chuckled while listening to him repent his sins. He and his fraternity brothers had defiled dozens of young ladies, convincing them to participate in gang bangs and never looking them in the face again.

"It's nothing that I haven't heard before, Brock. Trust me when I say that after tonight, your little frat boy escapades will look like child's play."

The room fell silent as I walked back towards the door. Brock needed me just as much as I needed him, but for very different reasons. I'd done this plenty of times to know he'd get into it, but a bitch boy like him would take some coercion.

"What's that sound, Mistress Esmerelda?"

"Oh, that's just fastening Elvis into my strap-on."

I waited for his virginal ass cheeks to stop shaking before slamming the door shut, upon which Brock's head lifted straight up.

***

Brock

If it hadn't been for the shackles, the sound of the slamming door would have scared me into falling off of the table. Mistress

Esmerelda enjoyed pushing my limits, and as I lay there waiting for Elvis, I regretted not leaving sooner.

This was not at all what I'd expected.

Sure, I assumed the dungeons would involve some sort of female domination. I didn't expect to be penetrated by a dildo that was almost as big as my own cock. The sound of the clock above me ticking only added to my anticipation of what was to come.

The sensation of her long, acrylic nail sliding into my asshole made my head shoot up again.

"Hmmm, I think we'll need to start off with a butt plug. Put your head back down and relax, Brock. I'm a professional, remember?"

"Yes, Mistress Esmerelda."

Images of the girl from the night before ran through my mind. Her asshole was practically gaped open, so if she could do it, then so could I.

Right?

A warm, tingling lubricant slid into my asshole, followed by the tip of a fat, glass butt plug.

"I would take a deep breath and let it out slowly." Regardless of what she said, I found it impossible to breathe at that moment.

"Look, Brock. I really don't care what you do, but it will make the transition easier for you. This isn't an order, but merely a suggestion."

I groaned with restraint as fear balled up in my belly. Just as I had expected, it was not a welcome sensation. It felt like a baseball trying to go inside of my asshole, even though I knew the butt plug was significantly smaller.

Relax, man. Just think about all of those prostate orgasms you'll soon be having.

She wrapped her arm around my hips to hold me in place. Not like there was any need to, of course. The shackles were so tight that I was starting to worry about my blood circulation. The butt plug slowly began to sink into the dark recesses of my anus, followed by a subtle popping sound that locked it into place.

"It feels like it's ripping me apart," I muttered with my legs shaking, still in a compromising position with no way out unless she allowed it. "But…but…"

"Go on, speak," Mistress Esmerelda replied, refusing to hide the excitement in her voice.

"Oddly good too."

I closed my eyes as she slowly slid the butt plug in and out, feeling the glass slide along the inside of my asshole. It was definitely a different experience. How many times had I jerked off and thought about playing with my asshole, only to chicken out? The longer the glass slid inside of me, the more cum built up in my ball sack until I thought I'd explode all over the red mattress.

Mistress Esmerelda popped the plug out in one quick motion and then quickly replaced it with the tip of Elvis before my asshole had a chance to close up.

"I'm going to give you every single inch of Elvis, Brock. No need to be wasteful. Unless, of course, you don't think you can handle it."

My mind told me to leave. Beg Mistress Esmerelda to remove the shackles, get dressed, and never return to the dungeons. Nobody would have to know I'd been here, especially my frat brothers back at the house. God, they would never let me live this down!

But my aching balls told me to keep going.

"I can handle it, Mistress Esmerelda. I'm a fucking man." It came out as more of a whisper than declaration, as the muscles in my legs shook." Pain brings…pleasure."

"You can say whatever you want. The only thing I see in front of me is a bitch in training. I know all about how you talk about women behind their backs. It's degrading and reprehensible. This is what they feel when you fuck them, you know." Mistress Esmerelda leaned her chest again my back as I felt her hot breath in my ear. "Even that girl from last night. Her ass didn't get that big overnight, you know."

With one quick thrust, Mistress Esmerelda shoved the rest of Elvis inside of my asshole. I cried out in pain and pleasure, torn between begging her to stop and insisting that she continue.

Elvis was buried deep with not a single inch spared. The feeling was an indescribable mix of joy and gratification. Mistress Esmerelda pulled it all the way out until the head rested against the outside of my asshole and then drove it back inside of me yet again.

At least there were no windows for anybody to sneak a peek into my first anal training session. As Mistress Esmerelda plowed into me, I was relieved that it was happening within a safe place and with a mistress who teased me into submission.

Still, I was beginning to feel the pain.

"It fucking hurts," I bellowed, my head turning slightly to see Mistress Esmerelda smiling through her mask. "How can it hurt and feel good at the same fucking time?"

"What did you think was going to happen? I'm sticking eight inches of rubber inside of you. There's going to be more pleasure coming your way, but you'll have to wait patiently for it to happen. I'm going to fuck the living daylights out of you. Just as you do to all of those sluts!" She mocked him with a deep seductive laugh…and I fucking loved it.

"You are a fucking bitch, and I'm going to make you pay for this!" I fumed with anger but arched my back for more. I liked this game. And so did she.

"The only fucking bitch in this room is you, Brock! Get used to it. Remember, you don't know me, but I know where you live. I'm going to let that sink in for a few moments while I have my fun with you. By the way, I'm not paying for anything. You're the one giving me cash to do this to you. I would be quick to remember that." Mistress Esmerelda spoke defiantly while giving me every fucking inch.

I breathed through the mix of pain and pleasure as she rammed into me, gripping onto the end of the red mattress with my shackled arms. "I forgot to mention," she said while maintaining velocity. "This is a squirting dildo!"

"What the fuck does that even mean?"

But she didn't answer me.

Instead, Mistress Esmerelda reached around and wrapped her hand around my thick, throbbing cock as she wiggled Elvis just slightly. The feel of her hot handset me off. My body began to convulse as cum pumped into her palm.

As my head collapsed onto the red mattress, I heard Mistress Esmerelda climax, followed by the sound of a trigger on the dildo. Warm, hot, creamy filling poured into my asshole, causing me to have yet another orgasm.

<u>Chapter Three</u>
Brock

I was filled with shame while leaving the dungeons that night, walking out to my car in the dark and hoping nobody could see me. A handful of streetlights lit up the otherwise dreary parking lot as I fumbled for my keys, slid them into the lock, and held my breath while sitting down.

My asshole had never felt so used.

As I drove back home, I thought about why I had agreed to meet with Mistress Esmerelda again in three weeks. My initial plan had been to compose myself and get the hell out of there, but that sexy receptionist's voice lured me in. The way she purred my name while opening up their appointment book made my cock stir again. But as I glanced down her exposed cleavage while scheduling my next session, I wasn't thinking about how good her nipples would taste in my mouth.

I was wondering what she'd look like with a strap-on around her waist, approaching me with Elvis as my ass cheeks were spread wide open.

"Fuck, I'm in over my head right now."

My car came to a slow stop as I pulled into our driveway. From the looks of things, my fraternity was having a party that evening. The last thing I wanted to do was talk with anyone that night, let alone a bunch of drunk college chicks trying to sleep with a fraternity guy.

Didn't they know how we made fun of them the next morning?

A handful of girls were hanging out on the front porch, clinging onto red plastic cups filled with alcohol as their short skirts revealed ass cheeks split in half by a thong.

My own ass cheeks clenched at the thought of *anything* being back there again.

One of the girls eyed me up and down with recognition as I walked along the pavement.

"Hey, Brock! We were just talking about you."

Her name also began with a B, and she had definitely faked her orgasm with me, but that's all I remembered.

"Hope you girls are having a good time tonight."

Long, acrylic nails ran along my forearm as I made my way inside the house, beckoning me to stay outside with them. I casually met their glances one by one, and you didn't have to be a rocket scientist to know what they had in mind.

A few weeks ago, my fraternity brothers and I had convinced some girls to have a mini-orgy. At the time, it was fun and definitely something to check off of my bucket list. But after experiencing Mistress Esmerelda have an actual orgasm while fucking my ass, as opposed to faking one with the hopes that I'd become her boyfriend, something had changed in me.

"You're not gonna join us tonight, Brock?"

The girl who spoke was pretty cute, with long black eyelashes that fluttered over eyes bluer slightly bluer than mine.

"I'm afraid not, ladies."

Her hand gravitated towards my ass, where she lightly patted it as I went inside the house.

I did my best to make small talk while filling a plastic bag with ice. The guys bought my lie about where I was that evening, even though part of me was dying to tell one of them. But I wanted to keep my session that evening to myself. Besides, they were busy trying to secure a fuck for the evening.

Thankfully, there wasn't anyone having sex in my bedroom.

For the first time in my life, I changed my own bedsheets and put away a pile of clothes that had been on the floor for a few days. And after a long, hot shower that helped ease the painful pleasure from Elvis, I went to bed as the rest of the house partied…with a bag full of ice cubes resting against my ass cheeks.

Chapter Four
Esmerelda

Aside from Brock and Hunter's rooms, the entire fraternity house was in desperate need of cleaning all over again. It was like I hadn't been there the last morning at all. They took no pride in their belongings. Underwear, t-shirts, condom wrappers, and bottles of booze were scattered throughout the entire place. This time, thankfully, there was no overpowering stench of body odor. It still lingered in certain areas but was slightly muted by the spray I had used the previous day.

It was a family recipe that was passed down from generation to generation. I was trying to get it patented with a lawyer whose payment came in free sessions. More money for me, and being fucked up the ass by Elvis for him. It was a win-win situation.

Knowing the frat boys would be speaking candidly in the dining area, devouring whatever high-carb snack they had picked up, I focused my attention in the nearby living room. Hunter was a no show, though. It was my suspicion that he probably got lucky and hadn't come home yet, although, from the looks of things, they'd had quite the party.

"So anyway, I was fucking this whore last night…I don't even remember her name. She was easy pickings at 2 AM, pretty wasted from the tequila shots. Anyway, after pumping away at her pussy for a while, of course, I came. A guy can only last so long, you know?" The guys nodded in agreement. "So, I dumped my load inside of her and, well…" Chet hesitated with a sigh of frustration.

"What happened?" Brock asked as if he were listening to the end of an epic tale.

"I don't know…the whore went crazy…started screaming that she was about to get off when I pulled out. She got fucked, though. What more did the bitch want from me?"

"Did you go down on her?" Brock asked.

"What kind of question is that, dude? That's gross. I wouldn't place my mouth anywhere near her fucking pussy. Besides, my dick was in there. I'm not fucking gay. I got what I wanted, and she could have joined me. She snoozes…she loses." Chet snickered while gulping the rest of his energy drink.

"I guess you're right. You know there *is* such a thing as foreplay, though." Brock insisted in a whisper.

Chet shrugged his shoulders while devouring another bite of his fast-food sausage biscuit meal.

"Foreplay? When did you become such a pussy, bro?" The other frat guys chuckled as Brock hung his head down, but not out of shame. *Good.*

Chet was eager to keep talking.

"Whatever. It's not like I'll fuck that slut again. Did I tell you guys about this cute little redhead in one of my classes? She's the shy and innocent type." Once again, everyone but Brock showed enthusiasm.

"I'm thinking about putting the moves on her. If I can get her drunk enough, maybe I'll share her with the rest of you. It's not like she'll notice she polished off an entire bottle of strawberry wine," he said with a playful jab to Brock's shoulder.

Brock just kept shifting uncomfortably in his chair, though, refusing to stoop back to their level.

That thing hanging between my legs indeed was a hunk of burning love.

Brock looked up as Chet stood, belching so loudly the walls nearly vibrated. "Bro, I'm all about getting some, but you should watch that shit with getting her drunk, man. It's kind of fucked up."

Chet paused and stared at his frat bro for a second. "I know, man. It's not like I'm fucking her after she's passed out. I didn't…mean…you know what I meant."

Brock nodded, and Chet waved his hands at him, rolling his eyes.

Chet stretched his long limbs over his head while walking out the back door, cracking his knuckles along the way. The white sleep pants did nothing to hide his natural attributes.

I wasted no time in heading upstairs to clean his room next, casually placing another business card on his desk.

***

Chet

The late-morning breeze brought in remnants of the night before. Cheap perfume mixed with alcohol filled my nostrils as I coughed, remembering all of the groups of girls who'd been dangling their heads off of the side of our wrap-around porch. Against my better judgment, I peered over to see if the cleaning staff had taken care of anything regurgitated.

Nope.

What the fuck are we paying them for, anyway?

I burst through the back door and peered into our community room, which was basically just a bunch of couches where we nursed our hangovers and a mattress. Except for that morning, everything had been turned upside down. Several cleaning staff members put the couches back together, dusting the windowsills, and holding their breath as they removed the sheets covered in questionable body fluids.

On second thought, they're doing a good job.

A cleaner exited my bedroom just as I was approaching. Despite being older than me, the woman was hot with a curvy body that I'd love to get my hands on. And whatever perfume she wore was a stark contrast to the cheap body sprays that I was used to smelling. It was a refined scent of rose mixed with vanilla.

Might as well get some homework done.

Earning my bachelor's degree was the first step towards becoming a medical doctor, and the thought of so much schooling often overwhelmed me. My homework load for the weekend was more than I even had time for, too. But as a self-professed party boy, I only had myself to blame.

A black business card peeked out at me from underneath my pencil cup:

The sharp corners poked into my skin as I held it in my hand. Surely this must be some kind of a joke, but who would do such a thing? I shared my room with another guy, but he was pretty strait-laced compared to the rest of us. In fact, I'd never even seen him with a woman.

I searched for the name of the business and address, but only a local business came up under a different name. Even searching 'Mistress Esmerelda' didn't yield anything aside from a handful of porn stars, which I doubt would do that kind of work on the side.

Not when the ones I found made millions of dollars.

Out of curiosity, I called the number on the back of the card.

"Thank you for calling The Dungeons. This is Celeste."

Celeste? Have I ever fucked a girl named Celeste?

"Um, hi. What, um, kind of business is this ma'am?"

Whoever 'Celeste' was, she sounded hot as fuck.

"Let me guess: you found a business card?" For the first time in my adult life, I found it impossible to talk with a woman. "It's exactly what you think it is, darlin'. Are you interested in the BDSM lifestyle?"

As she rattled off a list of what I could experience during a Mistress Esmerelda session, I did another internet search. But this time, it was for Female Domination.

I didn't know what to expect, but being aroused by an older, seductive woman putting me on my knees was not one of them. I had always been the one in charge, so why not turn the tables around and let a woman work her magic?

But the more links I clicked on, the more I decided that I'd challenge her. If this Mistress Esmerelda was such a professional, it would serve her right to submit to a real man for a change. No woman had ever turned down my cock.

"So," Celeste said, "would you like to make an appointment?"

"Absofuckinglutely."

Celeste turned out to be just as sexy as I'd anticipated, sitting behind the reception desk wearing a black and purple bustier.

"Hey, baby. I'm-"

"For starters, my name's not baby. And you're Chet, right?"

Most women showed a little more respect towards me, but I chalked it up to her, working in a BDSM dungeon and let it slide.

"Yes, that's right."

I could only assume that I was in the waiting room, which consisted of black and red leather couches. A massive, gothic-style chandelier with lit candles hovered in the room's center, and unfamiliar music played in the background.

"Mistress Esmerelda's ready for you, Chet. Third door on your left down the hallway."

"Thank you, ma'am."

Celeste smirked at me while filing her nails.

"Good luck, *Chet*."

Whatever was happening in the other two rooms was muffled by soundproof walls.

Damn. I really wanted to hear people getting fucked.

Mistress Esmerelda's black steel door swung open just as I was about to knock, and holy hell, was she a vixen. Wearing a devil-red, latex bodysuit, and matching thigh-high boots, it was no wonder she got men to submit.

"God damn, Mistress. I hope you're ready for me to fuck your brains out tonight," I announced confidently. A yelp escaped my lips as she yanked me by the collar, dragging me into her room and slamming the door shut behind me.

"I highly doubt Celeste told you that was on the menu for tonight. Regardless, have a seat so we can get started."

As Mistress Esmerelda locked the door, I quickly checked myself in a nearby mirror. Not that there was any point, of course. My military-style buzzcut hair never moved, and I was wearing simple jeans and a black t-shirt.

An uncomfortable steel chair was waiting for me in the center of the room, bolted to the floor. Mistress Esmerelda's hand on my chest prevented me from going towards it, though.

"Take off your clothes. I'm only going to ask you once. It would be in your best interest not to make me ask you a second time. Everything has to come off. And I do mean *everything*."

Despite being too horny to control the situation and put her in her place, I began to smell something very familiar. It was a high-end perfume with notes of rose and vanilla.

"Holy fucking shit! I know who you are!"

Mistress Esmerelda pushed me down onto the steel chair, causing my bare ass to wince in pain as she put her hand over my mouth.

"Don't you dare tell anyone, but yes, I'm one of the cleaners. There are twenty of us on staff. How did you know, though?" I didn't want to tell her, though. Instead, my mouth hung open as she rolled her eyes at me from behind the mask. "You are pathetic."

Mistress Esmerelda walked back and forth for a few minutes, studying my naked body from head to toe. Even if I wanted to leave, my fully-erect cock would never get back into my jeans without a proper release.

"What makes you think you are worthy of fucking me, Chet?" My head followed as she walked around me, turning back and forth to stare at her body beneath the tight red suit. "I think you'll find most women need more than penetration to get off. A man's tongue is a lethal weapon when it's used right. You don't know one thing about women, though, do you?

Her long leather boot pressed into my crotch, and for the first time, I realized that pain and pleasure can be experienced simultaneously. However, I was still terrified that she would do something to make me less than a man.

When I was about to object, however, she pressed her finger to my lips.

I flung my head away, deciding I'd had enough despite my obvious arousal.

" *You* take orders from *me,* Esmerelda. I'm paying through the nose to be with you tonight instead of finding some slutty, drunk college chick to fuck. And you know damn well that I'm not one of those beta male soy-boys, either. Maybe I'll lick you after I bust a nut on that pretty face of yours, at least the party that I can see. Unless, of course, I make you take the mask off."

Mistress Esmerelda smirked while slowly lowering her latex boot to the floor, and within a second, shackles wrapped around my ankles and wrists as she came within inches of my face. Her ruby-red lips were so close to mine that I could practically taste them, along with her intoxicating perfume.

"You are such a cocky little piece of shit, aren't you, Chet?"

Chapter Five
Esmerelda

Chet refused to look at me as he tried jumping out of the chair, only to be pulled back by the metal rings around his ankles and wrists.

"This room is full of buttons that I can push in an instant, Chet. And for such an Alpha male, you sure are coming off as weak and inferior right now. If you think shackles are scary, then how will you react at the pain of a thousand volts shooting throughout your body?"

Chet's eyes slowly widened as they turned to face me.

"What kind of sick, sadistic woman are you, Esmerelda?"

"You're about to find out, *Chet.*"

"Well, you can forget about having me fuck you after this shit! Hell, if I liked you enough, maybe we'd end up dating. I'm studying to become a doctor, you know."

I burst out laughing.

"You don't have the kind of balls I'm looking for in a partner, Chet."

I slowly dragged the heel of my boot along his red, swollen nuts.

I slid Elvis into my harness, swaying it back and forth in front of his eyes.

"I know you don't satisfy your partners, Chet. Regardless of your profession, no woman will stay faithful if you don't make her cum, you selfish piece of shit. Unless you're ready to listen to reason, my friend Elvis here will fuck some sense into you."

Chet's eyes stayed wide-open as he shook his head.

"I will do anything, Mistress Esmerelda. Just don't come anywhere near me with that thing," he snorted in derision.

"That's a good boy. This lesson will be better served on your back." The heel of my boot hit another button, thereby lowering the chair until it turned into a table. I stood over him with both heels on either side of his head until I was squatting into position.

"A man should know how to please a woman orally, *Chet*. You master this technique, and every woman will be begging to be with you. Stick out your tongue and let me see what I'm working with." My body slowly descended onto his face until he had no choice but to stretch out his tongue.

He wiped it over the leather of my crotch, making me tremble with a hungry need. My long, acrylic nails slowly pulled the zipper down to reveal my bald mound.

He looks disgusted. Silly boy.

"I'm going to let you in on a little secret, Chet. Ladies of a certain impressionable age don't like sucking cock; they only do it to please their partners. Some might get off on it, but most often, they're just going through the motions. There is power in eating pussy. Make them find that sweet release by going down on them, and they will do practically anything in return," I revealed.

I pressed against his shocked expression with my hot lips separating to feed his oral instrument into me. Chet was nothing more than a toy for my amusement, as my body bounced with my heels firmly planted on the floor.

"Don't just let me do all the work, boy!. You still have two good hands. I'm not going to give you a blueprint. It's up to you to figure these things out without my constant hand-holding," I said when I felt the fluttering end of his tongue.

His fingernails dug into my thighs and felt good. So good, in fact, that it nearly pushed me over the edge. So, I slowed him down when he got too close to the raging inferno of my orgasm simmering on the surface.

"There are always going to be highs and lows. When you find something that works, you don't stop until you see her eyes rolling into the back of her head. Every woman is different. You have to anticipate and watch closely for the signs. The way they sound and move are clear indicators. The twitching of their thighs will tell you that you are on the right path," I said with a pause, letting those words sink into his consciousness.

He wasn't paying attention to my clit and probably didn't even know where to find it. It was easy to direct his tongue until he finally got the idea. Wide circles of his tongue gave my body a much-needed bold of excitement, causing me to yip as I ground my cunt all over his fucking face.

It was Chet's moaning, however, that sent me over the edge.

The vibration traveled throughout my body, and within seconds I was screaming his name. My nails dug into his scalp as I foraged for a hair follicle, but his hair was too damn short. Nevertheless, I cried while squirting into his mouth, and it was nothing short of euphoric, with the radiation of warmth spreading through me like wildfire. I continued bucking with wild thrusts against his mouth.

You're not going anywhere.

My juices spilled down his chin and rolled down his neck.

After a few minutes of being in a comatose state of climactic pleasure, I struggled to my feet. My twitching fingers pressed a button to release him from the steel chair.

My hand slapped his away as he reached for his cock, ready to jerk off and shoot his load.

"What the fuck are you doing, Mistress Esmerelda?"

"On second thought, go ahead and jerk off for me, Chet."

His eyes lit back up as he got to work, hunching over while pumping away at his cock. At no point did he break eye contact with me, either.

"Fuck, Mistress Esmerelda! I'm getting close!"

"Stop touching yourself!"

Chet screamed out of frustration while letting go, and within a minute, his erection had gone down.

"Why the fuck did you ruin my orgasm?"

He reached for his cock to get it hard again, but I shoved his manhood into a chastity cage on there first.

"You have three weeks to think about what you have done in the past. There's no way out of that thing without a key, either." He stared at me in disbelief as I dangled the key on a string from my finger.

"What the fuck? I can't go three weeks without coming!"

"Well, there is something you can do, Chet. But it would require anal penetration." He held his hands up and shook his head defiantly. "That's what I thought. By the way, everything here has been recorded. I'm guessing you wouldn't want your brothers to know what you've done tonight," I giggled.

Chet almost tripped over himself, wiping his mouth with the back of his hand. He would not be able to have sex for three weeks unless it strictly pleased a woman with his mouth. Touching himself wasn't an option with the cage in place. He wouldn't want anybody to know about it, either. He would become a recluse until his next session in three weeks. Of course, I couldn't release any of the tapes, but the fear of it led to the pleasure building inside of him.

And the pleasure was precisely what he was going to get…eventually.

***

Chet

I sat in my SUV for several long, quiet minutes. How the hell had I succumbed to a woman like Mistress Esmerelda? Why did I plant my mouth on her pussy and eat her out? And why did I allow her to put this fucking chastity cage around my cock?

Because you wanted to do it, Chet.

I took a swig of my water and sped out of the parking lot. The night was still young, and there were bound to be plenty of drunk college chicks at the local bars. After high-fiving several acquaintances at my favorite one, I sat down at the bar and ordered a beer on tap.

And even though it was hidden underneath my jeans, I still felt like people somehow knew I was locked in chastity.

The brunette bartender winked at me while handing me the beer.

"I was wondering if you'd be here tonight, Chet."

I didn't know her name, but the two of us had flirted on several occasions. The only reason we hadn't fucked was that I was there all the time, and I had no intentions of ever dating the woman. But now that I was locked up in chastity, I found it easier to have a conversation with her.

"Yeah, I was just busy running errands and decided to cool off for a bit."

"Well, some of the girls have been asking about you."

Of course, they have, because my cock is nearly eleven inches long.

"I'm afraid I'm not here for that sort of thing tonight. Just looking to unwind, if you know what I mean."

While staring at her gorgeous, tanned cleavage, I felt my cock trying to get hard within my steel cage. It only got worse when she turned around and bent over, revealing that gorgeous ass whose cheeks were nearly popping out of her skirt. She was saying something to another bartender that made both of them giggle.

Why do I feel like they're laughing at me being in chastity?

"When do you get off-um…"

She leaned across the bar, proudly displaying the cleavage that had always gotten my attention.

"Barbara. My name is Barbara, Chet, and I'm off in about fifteen minutes. Wanna do something?"

I wanted to do a lot of things. Bend her over the bar and plow into her, maybe while she's eating another woman's cunt out. Pass her between my fraternity brothers and blow our loads in all of her holes.

And none of that was possible.

Yet, for some reason, I still wanted to spend time with her.

"Yes, Barbara. I'd love to do something."

About twenty minutes later, I had Barbara on her back in my car with her legs spread apart. Her cunt tasted just as good as Mistress Esmerelda's as I lapped her up, working my fingers in and out as she screamed my name. And to my surprise, my cock kept trying to get hard.

"Oh fuck, Chet! Right there! Suck on my clit!"

I did as I was told, sucking on her clit while burying my fingers deep inside of her cunt. That's all it took for her to cum, screaming my name and kicking her legs at the same time. And when it was all over, I declined her invitation for a blowjob and drove her home.

Despite not being able to get hard, my balls were aching and full of cum.

I thought about Mistress Esmerelda's recommendation about anal penetration. Even though I was put off by the idea of taking it up the ass, I went ahead and slid a finger up there while parking in front of Barbara's apartment building. I didn't think anything would happen.

But it did.

A long, loud scream shot out of my mouth as cum drooled out of my cock. It was my very first prostate orgasm, which caused every drop of semen to be expelled from my cock and balls.

Suddenly waiting three weeks didn't seem so hard, no pun intended.

<u>Chapter Six</u>
Esmerelda

Things were getting interesting between the frat boys and me. I had a feeling my work had only begun, though—the guys in the fraternity needed to know how their actions could make them pariahs. Girls talked, and word would spread quickly about what their tongues could do.

I was busy cleaning Hunter's room that morning, feeling a little relieved that I wasn't going to have to deal with his brotherhood's idea of living in squalor. Everything was in its place. Then again, that's to be expected from a man that had his shit together. And if his wardrobe was any indication, that trickled down to how he treated the ladies. Unlike the other guys in the house, he didn't dress like a cocky, self-entitled asshole.

There wasn't much to do except for some light dusting and cleaning the bathroom. Hunter's laptop was still on, though. Biting the inside of my cheek, I glanced down the hall to make sure it was empty before quietly closing his bedroom door. There was an arrow over a certain file, practically daring me to click on it.

My curiosity got the best of me.

I put on a pair of nearby headphones the second a video popped up.

"… I know you like it… you nasty little cunt. A whore like you needs to be used like this all the time, don't you? My boiling jizz is going to paint your whore face! And you better not wash it off before taking your walk of shame, you fucking slut!" Hunter was grunting from behind the camera, which was pointed down towards the poor girl's face.

I can't watch anymore! How dare he humiliate this young girl. She's not into it at all! All she wants to do is please him.

I could tell on her face that she didn't like being the subject of his masculine ridicule. Although I didn't watch long enough to see him ejaculating, the words were strictly for his pleasure.

I stood there mortified, wondering how I could be so wrong about Hunter. It finally dawned on me that he was the worst of the three of them. He was pretending to be this paragon of virtue. He had me fooled, but hadn't I always known there was something off that I couldn't quite put my finger on? It was probably the same way the girls felt when he flirted with them shamelessly, never giving up until he had them alone in his room.

It's an act. How could I be so stupid when I knew better?

In a knee-jerk reaction, I shamelessly transferred all the files to my email address. It served him right after putting on this air of innocence around me and the other girls in my company. One of my employees had mentioned in passing that he had asked her out, too.

I encouraged her to take a risk, telling her that he was the last of the good ones.

I walked away, but not before I left my calling card next to his laptop. If Hunter got off on humiliating women, then let's see how he reacts to being humiliated.

I took one last look at his picture in the frame where he was smiling for the camera. He made the good ones look bad, that's for damn sure.

As I made my way downstairs, I could hear all of the fraternity boys laughing. They were playing beer pong in the dining room, talking about spending the day getting wasted and drinking their worries away. It would've been fun to beat them at a game they thought they were better at, but that would have shone a light on me, which was the last thing I wanted to do.

Tonight is going to be something special just for Hunter.

***

Hunter

The fraternity house smelled like beer and bad decisions that afternoon when I came back with several bags of groceries. As head of the house, it was my job to keep the kitchen stocked with food and beverages. It was an easy enough gig, except I wish my frat brothers would have consumed more water than beer.

"How the fuck can you guys get so wasted during the day?"

None of them answered me, though. They were busy playing video games in our living room, yelling obscenities between shoving fists of unhealthy snacks into their mouths. I thought about chucking some apples their way, but it would have been a waste of good fruit.

"Hey yo, Hunter, why don't you join us, man?"

"Nah, I'm good, bro. Gonna get in a nap before we party tonight. Maybe catch up on some homework, too."

"Suit yourself."

I jogged upstairs a few minutes later, eager to be alone with my laptop and a bottle of lubrication. My latest video had been of some whore I ran into at a bar while my brothers were partying at home. I had convinced her to come back home with me, where I filmed myself jerking off on her face.

And because it was a point of view video, I could upload it to porn sites and make money without anyone knowing it had come from me. There was no way that my father, who was an elected official in Washington, D.C., would ever find out.

But when I pulled my laptop over to my bed for a masturbation session, a black business card fell to the ground:

The Dungeons ~ Anything Goes ~ Mistress Esmerelda

Fear ran through my body as I thought that I'd been exposed. But how?

Something wasn't adding up.

Curiosity sunk in the longer I looked at the business card, but I didn't want anything traced to my cellphone or IP address. Instead, I hopped into my car and went for a drive, where I conveniently ended up outside a local business with the same address as The Dungeons.

People were coming and going from the store, which meant The Dungeons was probably in the basement. I thought about just going down there myself, but surely nobody could be there during the daytime.

A woman looked over at me from a nearby parked car, then winked at me with a smile on her face.

Just call the number on the card, you fucking pussy.

Following my intuition, I did just that and watched as the woman a few cars down picked up the phone. A short while later, I hung up the phone with some woman named Celeste and had a standing appointment that evening with Mistress Esmerelda.

If I could film myself cumming all over a Dominatrix's face, then I'd be looking at one massive payday.

***

Esmerelda

With Celeste's help, my plan for Hunter was quickly coming together.

"This is not like you, Esmerelda, and I have to wonder why the change of heart. You're seriously going to share a man with me tonight?"

"Yes, Celeste. Why does that surprise you so much?"

"It's just that the others are talking about you in rave reviews. They tell me in confidence that you have come a long way in your quest to be a dominatrix. Missy was the first to give you her seal of approval, you know. That's not easy to get, and you should feel grateful she thought that you were worthy of such an honor," Celeste announced behind her desk, typing furiously.

"I'll give you a call when I'm ready," I said with the key around my neck, swinging back and forth underneath my clothing.

I knew it was there, but it stayed in the shadows where it belonged until I was ready for it. Every night I could find that calming influence by slipping the key into the lock and hearing the click that followed.

This time I dressed so that Hunter would know to kneel in my presence when he saw me. The light blinked to signify that he was on his way, too. My black leather skirt went down to my ankles with a long, revealing slit up the side to my inner thighs.

The black bustier gave the allusion I was going to have a wardrobe malfunction, though. It seemed gravity was going to lose the battle without the double-sided tape to keep them in place. The mask had glowing red eyes with an open mouth so that my tongue could protrude with minimal effort.

There was no way that I would be able to kiss away the pain after I inflicted it. This was going to be emotionally scarring. There were many ways to dominate, physically, and emotionally. They both held a different degree of control over my subjects.

I stood with my back toward him and my arms crossed when the door opened.

"Don't say a word. I want to know what you fantasize about when nobody else is looking. Tell me what your fetishes are, Hunter. Say anything else, and you will be requested to leave with physical force." I stated an ultimatum to give him no wiggle room to ask any questions.

"I'm not sure this is where I should be," Hunter stammered without moving from the spot that he was in.

"I think you are exactly where you need to be. I feel the heat of your libido from across the room. Don't you want the opportunity to find that elusive orgasm that men are afraid to talk about? It can be liberating. You never know what might happen if you stay. It's a risk, but a calculated one. Can you really walk away from all this?" I asked and spun on my heels to face him in my attire, which he couldn't seem to take his eyes off of.

"You are stunning," he stammered with just a hint of his tongue coming out of his mouth.

"I don't need your damn praise. I'm not some airhead. I asked you a question, and I expect an answer," I pressed with the riding crop against his chest, snapping one of his buttons.

He jumped every time another button came loose to reveal his muscular chest. Grabbing his belt and pulling him toward me was met with little resistance. Taking off his belt and restraining his hands behind his back would prevent him from walking out the door. I pulled down his zipper and reached inside to tantalize his body and mind, with my fingers walking freely up and down his shaft. His moan gave me all the encouragement I needed to continue. The feeling of him throbbing was a good indication he was under my thumb.

"I-I, um, like to humiliate women. I enjoy it and get off knowing they are ridiculed by their friends," he admitted with a catch in his throat. "But please don't tell anyone!"

"Why not, Hunter?"

"Because my father is a congressman!"

This is going to be so much fun.

<u>Chapter Seven</u>
Esmerelda

"I want you to feel what those girls go through every time you do that. This is one of my tools," I referred to the lipstick in crimson red.

I found inspiration from the words spoken to me before I had shed my timid skin. I scrawled several dirty words on his body, pressing hard into his chiseled flesh. It would come off with a lot of scrubbing. **Whore** was written on his forehead. His chest was emblazoned with the word **Slut**. **Bitch** was written on his right leg. **Used** on his left leg and **Abused** on his right arm. **Pig** was then scrawled on his back and **Open for Business** on his butt cheeks.

It's a masterpiece in desperate need of an audience.

"Take hold of that thing in both hands and stroke it for me. Stroke it for us," I hinted, unfastening his hands, without him fully comprehending until he heard the footsteps of others in the room.

There were five in total from other rooms in the dungeon that had taken time out of their busy schedule to work with me. It didn't happen often but could be quite beneficial.

He stood there staring at us, all dressed in various leather pieces with strategic areas exposed for his pleasure. Celeste was the first to speak on behalf of the others. She'd spoken often of getting out of the business, but it always seemed to lure her back in. It was in her blood. She had a legacy of dominating after being raised by two women with a penchant for violence against men.

"Look at the little pig. What's the matter, little piglet? You don't have anything that we haven't seen before. You're a little slut, crying out for dripping hot cock. I can see you on your knees, giving your fraternity brothers that mouth. Bending over and spreading those cheeks for all the boys to use and abuse until you're filled with their nasty loads." She spoke with little bits of spittle flying from her mouth onto his face.

"Is that what you are? I believe Mrs. Celeste has pegged you. I mean, she hasn't yet, but the night is young. She would get a thrill out of fucking you so hard that you'd be screaming for your mommy." I belittled him while watching him stroke faster.

The others began to call out taunts.

"He looks excited, but I can't be sure when I have to squint to see it."

"I bet he'd look good in a skirt, taking it up the ass from behind while I pulled his hair."

"You should be ashamed of yourself for jerking off in front of us like this. What are you waiting for?"

He hears the voices ridiculing him. I can see that he's ashamed... but there's something else going on. He loves it. There's no hiding it.

"Come for us... Come for us... Come for us... Come for us..." Those three words got louder until he was shaking all over.

He grunted, his neck muscles pronounced, and then fired a warning shot across the bow of my boot. It splattered against our feet until his legs turned to jelly. He dropped to his knees with his head down and his body heaving with every breath.

I grabbed his hair and made him look at all of us. "You are a worm. This is done for tonight. You ruined it by prematurely finding your release. The punishment for this disobedience is a repeat session in three weeks. Don't even think about saying anything. Get your clothes and get out before I let them have their sadistic fun with you."

I clapped my hands to get him to move. He didn't slow down until he was scrambling up the stairs.

I turned to the others, and we all smiled, knowing full well he'd be back.

***

Hunter

I'm surprised I didn't trip over my two feet, running out of that place.

Someone was onto me, but who? Did someone from the porn websites, a woman, figure me out and send these Mistresses after me? Whatever the reason was, I knew what needed to be done regardless of who did it.

As soon as I got home, I immediately deleted all of the videos I'd uploaded on every adult website. There were dozens of them, too. All of which featured girls I didn't even remember taking loads of my cum all over their faces.

As I looked at every video I'd uploaded, I could no longer deny that they didn't enjoy doing it.

At the time, I'd convinced myself that they were into it. They got off on *being* humiliated just as much as I got off on humiliating *them*. But I wasn't fooling anybody. I knew damn well the only people who'd watch those videos would be men like me, who believed that women were supposed to service men, whether it was in the bedroom or the kitchen.

But not anymore.

After removing and deleting every single video I'd uploaded, I cashed out all of my porn royalties. Nearly three-thousand dollars was headed toward my bank account, and I was riddled with guilt. I didn't deserve a fucking penny of that money, but I also didn't want to admit to what I'd done.

I thought about calling an emergency meeting to discuss changing how we ran things at the fraternity house, but that would bring too much attention to myself. My frat brothers would wonder what the hell had gotten into me, and even though I was a changed man, I had to keep up the facade.

I took a long, hot shower and went to bed long before that evening's fraternity party got started. I also bolted my bedroom door shut and told the guys that I wasn't feeling well.

My slut-shaming days were now behind me.

***

Esmerelda

The line in the invisible sand had been crossed, and there was no going back.

I had barely begun to explore the deepest recesses of their minds. There was an amazing transformation afoot, with little talk about conquests around the dining room table that morning. I made it my business to listen in earlier when I was cleaning and found it amusing to find they were not basking in the notches on their bedposts for once.

However, I had found something unusual in Brock's room that would come up in conversation when we met later that night. A double-headed black dildo was underneath his mattress, recently used.

He had become a slave to his anal desires and had me to thank for it. I would need to have a class on proper dildo hygiene, though, given the smell of the room.

The dungeon was completely prepared for his imminent arrival that evening, an hour before his appointment time. I had gone out of my way to acquire the exact same dildo underneath his mattress. There were several of them hanging from the ceiling. The clerk behind the counter at the sex shop down the street was a little too curious. She probably thought I was going to have an orgy, but this was a party for two.

"I have to tell you last night awakened something inside of me. I thought I was done with this. There wasn't anything more I could do, but I stand corrected. I'm going to begin seeing clients in the last remaining room in the dungeon. I blame you for making me see what I have been missing by depriving myself of dominating a man into submission. I want to give you this." She offered an antique mask circa the 1800s.

"I can't accept this. It must be worth a fortune to a collector," I gasped, running my fingers over the beautiful etchings.

It was quite fragile and brittle from age.

"My parents encouraged me to give it to you. They were quite tickled to learn that I was getting back into the business. They never understood why I took a step back. You have earned my respect and admiration. I should let you get back to it. Brock should be here in a few moments. I will send him to you. Do you think that I can watch?" she asked, with a motion of her eyes toward the camera that was inert.

"That would be a great idea. I usually record everything, but there's no reason why I can't transmit the video to the other rooms. You will have to have your clients sign a nondisclosure agreement to gain access to the live video. I don't think it's unreasonable for the rest of you to provide a suitable donation in whatever nomination you think is fair." I suggested, with thoughts of complimenting my income with a little more on the top.

"I will have a talk with the others and see what we can come up with. You'll have the nondisclosure agreements signed and delivered to your private email within the hour. We can use your video as a teaching aid for those that are still novices in this trade," she pointed out.

I was perfectly fine with it, but only under the pretense that the mask had to stay on the entire time. The same couldn't be said for my clients. What they didn't know wasn't going to hurt them. Everybody had a lot to lose and nothing to gain by making the videos public. We had a business to run and needed the anonymity to keep our clients happy. We would blur his face out anyway.

I heard him behind me and turned to see him darting his eyes around the room with a surprised expression on his face. While he was in a state of conscious shock, I took the liberty of removing his shirt and pants before using a pair of scissors to slice his underwear.

"What the fuck?"

I ignored Brock's question and moved forward with my mission, removing the underwear with two quick snips on either side. He was naked within seconds.

I slapped his ass with the double-headed black dildo in my hands. Brock jumped at the cold, black rubber material running down the crack of his ass.

This is what it feels like to have the power. I want more of it. He's giving in....but I like to see him fight with those eyes on fire. His anger is there, only tempered with a bit of humility.

"Somebody has been a naughty boy. You don't have to say anything though, Brock. A little birdie told me about your latest acquisition. You love getting fucked up the ass now, don't you?" Brock nodded enthusiastically while beads of sweat trickled down his face. "The very thought of getting fucked again wakes you up in the middle of the night, wishing that I was standing at the foot of your bed holding onto Elvis. He's taking the night off. Don't worry though, I have a suitable replacement," I revealed with a wicked sneer on my face.

His eyes lit up upon seeing the massive, black dildo.

"I bought one after our first session and haven't been able to stop using it ever since. I like it better than fucking women, Mistress Esmerelda. Although, I do miss making them eat my cum. What have you done to me, Mistress?" he pleaded with his voice cracking.

"I opened you up to the possibilities literally and figuratively. I have been more than lenient. I thought I made myself clear about how you can only speak with my permission. I'm sure you do miss having them on their knees, sucking your cock until you fill their mouth. Do you ever think they might be squeamish about swallowing?" I asked with my finger pressing hard into his bare chest.

" Of course… I mean…who wants to eat cum? It's so fucking hot when I make them do it by holding their head with both hands, though," he confessed.

"I'm going to be using Brutus the Black Dildo. Take a look at it from every angle. I want you to fully realize what is going to be inside of you." I snickered while brandishing the weapon of mass destruction. It was thicker and longer than the one he had used on himself.

"I can't take something like that," he yelped.

I cracked my whip on the floor, reprimanding him for speaking out of turn.

"I'll make it fit. Assume the position with your hands on the wall, and get ready for the fuck of your life!"

Chapter Nine
Esmerelda

I directed him to the cold and unforgiving brick wall before lubricating the giant phallus protruding from my crotch. The light vibration was the perfect incentive to have him squealing like a pig.

He's vulnerable. I'm feeling magnanimous.

With my leather-clad fingers covered in petroleum jelly, I slid two fingers deep into his rectum. I watched him go from squirming to completely motionless.

"I'm not going to be the one fucking you. You're going to do that for me. This is called a pocket pussy. It's attached to the wall in front of you. I'm sure you've used them before, though, since you're a horny little fuck. Just remember, once you're inside, Brutus is behind you, waiting for his turn. He's going to be the next thing you feel when you pull out of it." I explained the process with both hands wrapped around Brutus, keeping it in place.

Come on…curiosity only kills cats…

I watched over his shoulder as he tentatively stuck his head into the makeshift pussy. It was already slick with lubrication to give him the proper push in the right direction. He felt those lips close in around him, and he began feeding the pocket pussy one inch at a time.

"I want you to tell me how it feels," I whispered into his ear before biting it hard enough to make him scream.

He wailed and then grunted his response. "God damn you…it doesn't feel like the real thing. It is snug and very hot…Oh God… it's massaging every inch!"

"What are you waiting for? Don't tell me you're scared of Big Brutus. He's nothing more than a gentle giant with an addiction to fucking men until they're crying. The only thing he wants is your asshole, Brock!" I urged for his compliance with the camera recording his emotional struggle for everybody to see in the dungeon.

He began to press back with the head wedged in between his ass cheeks. I was continually adding more lubrication with a squirt bottle that ran down along the length of that monstrosity. It finally popped through the resistance with his head snapping back at the implication of what that meant.

His cock was barely half out of the pocket pussy. Everybody watched to see what he was going to do next, probably on the edge of their seats. They were dying to see him have every single inch buried inside of him.

"You can do better than that. I might even let you release a boiling load, if you're lucky! That's depending on whether or not you are a good boy for me. I want you to take the whole thing. I know you don't think it's possible, but I can assure you, it is. I promised Big Brutus a good time, and I'm not gonna disappoint him."

I never took into account that his cock was not as long as the one around my waist. He was able to fuck the pocket pussy with rapid strokes and only take half of the one that was strapped around my waist. It wasn't good enough, which meant I was going to have to take matters into my own hands.

I grabbed his hips and prepared to let Brutus give him the business. His passionate scream made my entire body quiver with trembling desire. My nipples instantly went hard as my own lubrication traveled down between my pussy lips. I banged him without mercy, opening up his asshole to receive the gift I was bestowing upon him.

"You have taken every single inch of this twelve-inch monster. I'm guessing your head feels like it's going to explode. You have my permission to let it happen. I'm going to continue to fuck you until you finish inside of that thing. The more you wait, the more I'm going to fuck you with this thing," I threatened, continuing to move my hips forward and back, my legs screaming at me the entire time.

It was a taste of what men went through when they had to do all the work. I had a newfound respect for their stamina. It didn't stop me from ripping him a new one, though.

"I think you need a little more to push you over the edge, but you're not going to get it from me. I have all night. I think it goes without saying that Big Brutus doesn't need to rest in order to recharge his batteries. Oh, wait, I almost forgot," I said before reaching around to press the button on the pocket pussy.

It initiated the vibration portion around the lips that traveled throughout the contraption. I also doubled that vibration by initializing the same function on the dildo inside of him. It was priceless to see his body react, and he screamed when he unloaded what probably felt like a gallon of cream into the reservoir.

I pulled out as he slowly sank to his knees, absolutely exhausted from the ordeal.

Giving after I had taken so much, I sat down and coddled him against my breast for a few moments. Just long enough to let the residual pain reside and the trust to fold back into me.

"You're not done yet. You made a mess. I want you to clean it up."

He nodded and gripped the pocket pussy, lifting it from the wall. His eyes shifted toward me, then down to my pussy. Pursing my lips, I pulled them wide apart and grabbed his free hand, pulling it toward me. He pushed three fingers inside of me, and I squealed in delight. Unknowingly, he gripped the bottom of the pocket pussy, squeezing his warm cum all over his hand. I took the reins and lifted my hips, moving forward and back, fucking his fingers.

With the feeling of his warm seed spilling down over my leg, I came hard, my juices covering his hand. My body twitched, and I smiled, giving it one last twist of my hips before pulling his hand back.

"Come back in three weeks. I'm going to have something special in store for you," I hinted, watching him crawl across the floor to gather up his clothes.

The remnants of his underwear was left behind.

I laid there with a smile, glancing up at the camera.

Chet was next on my hit parade. Things were working out better than I expected.

The guys had no idea which one of the cleaning crew was using them. Nobody was talking, but I could see them watching us out of the corner of their eyes every time we cleaned.

Not only was everybody on their best behavior, but their rooms were unusually tidy. We were getting paid the same amount to basically dust.

Each one required a different set of skills from me. Chet still had much to learn about what made a woman tick. He really didn't care, but I was teaching him the finer points of seduction. Oral sex was important, but foreplay took center stage.

Listening was the key. It was fun walking amongst them, wearing the key to their salvation around my neck, out of sight and out of mind. I closed my eyes and saw them on their knees, taking their punishment and swallowing their medicine in the form of hot cream dripping from their lips.

The idea was to treat them to my own special form of therapy. A one on one session was necessary to break them of their habits. It was starting to take hold in their minds how they had neglected the opposite sex. Cracking the code of their chauvinistic attitude was my greatest achievement.

Even when I entered into the Dungeon, readying for the night, my pride beamed. Men were interesting creatures. There was no doubt in my mind that half of them went back to their old ways when they stopped their sessions, but these three…I felt like it was different for them. Like they were being taught something they hadn't even realized to be true.

I walked out into the waiting room at The Dungeons just as another Mistress was walking inside.

"I just wanted to stop by and tell you how much I enjoyed your show last night. My client paid me a massive bonus to let him watch. I'm getting referrals. I think you deserve a finder's fee. I'm learning a lot from watching you," Mistress Emily enthused with a smile on her face.

"We have to stick together. Each one of us has a different skill set. There's no reason why we can't learn from one another. I suggest a quid pro quo, though. My videos in return for videos you make of your clients. We take turns in transmitting live feeds from the rooms each night. That way, we all benefit from the experience," I suggested while trying in vain to pull the zipper up from the back of my leather catsuit.

"That's a great idea. I have a different client coming in. He will be wearing a mask to hide his identity. That is a mandatory requirement in his case. He lives in the public eye under the scrutiny of a microscope concerning everything he does. I think that he would get a kick out of having our sessions shared with the other rooms. He's what I call a closet voyeur with mommy issues," she said with a chuckle, helping me pull up the zipper very slowly, her hot breath on my spine.

I suddenly felt her tongue following the trajectory of the zipper to the nape of my neck. It felt amazing. The softness of her lips touching me and the feel of her experienced tongue in the art of lesbian love was enough to set fire to my loins.

This is different. I can't say that I've ever been kissed like this.

"I'm guessing from your reaction that you've never been with a woman. It might be something you should think about. I am more than happy to volunteer my services for free. It's easy to open up to you. It's one of the reasons why you make a great dominatrix. I'm just getting my feet wet. I've always been partial to the female form," She admitted in a whisper that sent shivers down my spine.

Her perfume was intoxicating but didn't compare to her voluptuous curves. I started to think about running my hands over her body and then sticking my head between her thighs, with her knees pressed against my ears.

I was a little flummoxed and couldn't say a word to argue the point. Her gentle touch and the liquid heat of her tongue touching me were twisting my thoughts. I wasn't much for experimentation when I was younger, but that life reminded me we only had one chance to try new things.

"Don't be surprised if I take you up on your offer," I replied breathlessly.

"The invitation is open-ended. This fiery redhead would be glad to show you what you've been missing. I'm sure you can introduce this new aspect into your play. Just look for a window of opportunity and don't let it slip through your fingers," she warned with a seductive stare.

"I hope I'm not interrupting." She and I looked up to see Chet staring at us with a big grin on his face.

Mistress Emily kissed my cheek before excusing herself from The Dungeons, leaving just me and Chet alone in the waiting room.

Chapter Ten
Esmerelda

"Good evening, Chet. Follow me."

We walked down the hallway and into my room, where I promptly slammed the door once he was inside.

"You know the routine. I don't think you need a refresher course, although it did take a lot for you to make me orgasm with your tongue. I neglected one important detail from your sexual education," I said with the words hanging in the air while he stripped off his clothes.

"What's that?" Chet asked, his eyebrow raised.

"It's come to my attention that you're in love with yourself. How many mirrors do you need in your room? You can see yourself from every angle. That's a mortal sin... vanity. Loving yourself is important, but not as important as knowing what buttons to push to make a woman scream with unrestrained pleasure. That is your task today."

I stripped down to nothing, only wearing the antique mask made of wood.

He stayed standing at attention with his hands behind his back, the cage in place.

I provided the key and released him from it.

Look, his cock is timid now. Come on...I won't bite...hard.

"Women are afraid to say what they want in the bedroom. They want their man to know what to do. How can they when every woman is different? Being a good listener is important. Recognizing the signs of arousal and excitement will help you. I'm going to lie down on this black table, and you're going to do everything in your power to bring me that all-encompassing orgasm. You'll know when you see it," I stated, my body prone, lying there waiting to see how he was going to respond to my challenge.

Chet stood over me and walked around the table, committing my naked body to his memory. He now had the fortune of being able to close his eyes and imagine me naked whenever he desired, day or night.

"I'm going to give you a hint. Gentle waves of persuasion will slowly build with pressure. Take your time and get to know every part of me. Don't just concentrate on the main areas. There are other hot spots, including the back of my knees and my neck. That is the only cheat sheet you are going to get," I announced.

"I feel like a kid in a candy store. I don't know where to begin, Mistress Esmerelda. I suppose it all starts with a kiss," Chet said with his right hand cupping my head and bringing his lips closer until we were lip locked.

His technique was pretty good but still needed fine-tuning, including how he was darting his tongue in and out of my mouth. I showed him the right way, and he followed directions without verbal commands. He mimicked what I was doing and was soon igniting the nerve endings at the top of my mouth.

I squirmed when his fingers glided gently along my skin, briefly making contact with my nipples.

He was learning that subtlety was the answer to what it took to get a woman off.

He bit my lip and trailed his tongue in circles around my neck, making my legs kick out in response. My entire body jerked when his finger slid through my pulsing pussy lips and briefly penetrated but quickly pulled back.

"I think somebody is having way too much fun. Don't stop now. I'm curious to see where this goes," I said, my eyes watching his cock to see that it hadn't wavered from its ramrod condition.

He was so focused on teasing me that he wasn't consciously aware of his excitement. It was leaking profusely, and it throbbed with a desperate need to jettison what was inside.

"This is a first for me. I'm usually anxious to just hit it and quit it. I'm getting to know you intimately on a different level than I have ever done with any other woman. I find it fascinating to see what little things make you jump out of your skin. I'm watching every single detail, including the way you lick your lips when you don't think I notice." He slid his hands over my ankles and down, massaging my feet, pressing into the crevices.

I sighed with contentment as he climbed my calves. He tickled the back of my knees with both hands. He kissed my skin, my flesh trembling, begging for him to open the gates of my arousal.

He wasn't even touching himself, but his cock was bobbing up and down with affirmative action. He avoided the apex of my thighs and dipped his tongue into my navel, sending an electrical charge between my legs. His eyes conveyed a fascination for my pleasure that went beyond his need to please himself.

"You are a quick study. I think somebody has been researching the subject matter at hand. I'm impressed that you went to these…wow…lengths," I moaned, my upper body arching.

He suddenly latched onto my clit, which was already quite pronounced.

I was so close, but the added incentive of his fingers gently pinching my nipples sent me over the edge. He plunged three fingers into my quivering recesses. I was squirting all over the table and against his face. The way that he was twisting his fingers gave me no other choice than to have multiple orgasms at his hands.

I was literally convulsing and thrashing on the table when I felt his hot load shoot from the end of his prick. It landed hotly in wild streaks across my body. I could feel the heat and see the hot cream on my skin. I ran my fingers through the sticky mixture.

It was 30 minutes of complete bliss.

I grabbed the back of his neck and pulled his ear down to me. "Be back in three weeks. I have a big surprise for you."

The building blocks are there. I can't let on what I have planned. It's killing me to stay silent.

Chapter Eleven
Esmerelda

I sat in the break room, listening to everyone talk about their latest sessions with their clients. It became an open forum to discuss matters in a private space. It was my suggestion, and it was met with wild enthusiasm from the rest of the Mistresses. It gave us the chance to learn from those that had been down that road before.

I might've been experienced, but I still had a desire to learn more. To stretch myself creatively would give me wings. I could listen without judgment, and they could share their stories in a safe place without condemnation.

"All of you know that last night was my first session in almost five years. I came here strictly in an ownership capacity. I had a young man worshiping at my feet, licking my toes, and shooting his load all over them. His fetish gave me the unexpected bonus of creaming down my legs." Celeste detailed her experience with a young novice getting the first taste of his fetish without resorting to watching it online.

It was always a life-altering experience. They were finally in the spotlight at the feet of their Mistress. Some people called the rooms in the dungeon chambers of horror. That couldn't be further from the truth.

I chimed in. "I must admit that I've never been acquainted with that fetish. There's always a first time for everything. I like knowing I can learn new things. I think if somebody had told me a few years ago that I would be dominating men for money, I would have laughed in their faces. Speaking of humiliation, I believe I have a proposal for the rest of you."

"I'm sure this has something to do with the young man jerking off for us a couple of weeks ago. That was fun. I've wondered what you were gonna do to top it. I see you've already been thinking about that," Emily stated.

"It just so happens, he will be here in about one minute. I want all of you, including those that you dominate, to be here to witness his humiliation. I sent him a few items. He was told not to leave the house without wearing them in public. It's going to be interesting to see if he followed my directions to the letter."

Hunter walked into the dungeon wearing the black leather skirt and nothing underneath. It was comical to see him balance in 4-inch red pumps without falling flat on his face. The blond wig and clean-shaven features made him look like a passable girl in the right light.

"That is my good bitch showing up on time wearing what I sent you. Take a bow and walk around, introducing yourself to the others. Tell them exactly what I told you to say. Don't look at me like that. I want to hear the words," I urged with a motion of my hand for him to circle the room.

"I'm a nasty little whore hungry for…boiling cum all over my face.

This little girl wants all of her holes plugged. I'm at the mercy of Mistress Esmeralda. She controls me, and I do what she tells me without question. I'm on my knees, begging to be used. I'm a sniveling bitch thirsty for warm cum," he said before dropping to his knees and taking off the skirt to reveal his cock and balls were shaved bare at my request.

Those in attendance laughed when they saw that his cock was taped behind him. He looked like a woman from the waist down. His legs were shaved once again at my urging. His humiliation had taken an unexpected turn. I was amazed that he was willing to go through with it without any objections.

"Look at them and tell them how it makes you feel to be on your knees in front of them. They can already tell that it excites you. I would love for some man to provide you with a different kind of lipstick. I wonder if I could impose on one of their clients." I directed my comment to the other Mistresses standing in front of the table.

His body was smooth, including his armpits. The only remaining hair was on his head.

"I feel pretty… I feel like dancing," he said before getting up and moving around the room doing ballet with leaps into the air.

Surprisingly, his cock remained taped to his leg with industrial-strength adhesive.

They slapped his ass and pinched those cheeks until they were candy apple red. Their fingerprints were emblazoned on his skin, temporarily marking his flesh.

Nobody mentioned anything about a donor to paint his lips. Emily offered a dog leash, which I gratefully accept. I was anxious to put it on him.

"Have you been degrading women since our last meeting?" I asked with a snap of the leather leash, just licking his backside to make him answer truthfully.

"I haven't been with a woman since our first session. I lock my door and constantly masturbate to humiliation pornography. It's the only thing that gets me excited," he confessed to the laughter of his audience.

"Does that turn you on more than fucking women?" I asked with my arms crossed, waiting for his reply.

"Yes…yes, it does," he squeaked, returning to his knees in the center of the room.

I advanced on his position and showed him the blood-red ball gag before attaching it to his head. His mouth had to stretch to accommodate it, with his teeth digging into the pliable rubber ball.

The leash attained from Emily was the next piece of the puzzle.

I paraded him through the room on his hands and knees to kiss the feet of the Mistresses. He was groveling for my pleasure and gratification.

"I want to jerk off for all of you," he mumbled under his breath.

I paused and tilted my head to the side, then released the ball gag.

"I'm sorry, but you're going to have to speak up for everybody to hear you. Say it in a nice clear, and loud voice. This is your shame. I want you to relish in it," I advised.

"I want to jerk off for all of you and shoot my load at your feet. Please, let me do this… I'm begging you on my knees," he pleaded with his hands cupped together.

The awkward silence was the perfect aphrodisiac to keep him on pins and needles. He had no idea if I was going to give him permission. Being patient wasn't easy for him. His fingers were trembling. His lower lip was quivering, most likely angry at himself for begging to touch his cock.

"You want to put a show on for all of us. I will have to take the tape off. I believe in the old adage of ripping it off fast. Let me show you what I mean," I addressed before reaching out and grabbing it with one hand.

His eyes widened with everybody coming closer to watch the end result. I pulled, and he resisted the urge to scream by biting his bottom lip. There were hairs on the tape that had been taken out by the root. It was his fault for not shaving the area before attaching the tape.

"You have the undivided attention of everybody in the room. I'm not going to give you any further direction. I will stop you if I think you're not giving us your best. You'll be made to leave naked and shivering to a waiting taxi idling at the curb. The taxi driver has been paid to take you back to the fraternity house. Whether you are wearing clothes or not is entirely up to what happens here." I warned that his humiliation would be public knowledge with his friends watching him take that walk of shame.

He grabbed a bottle of baby oil lying on the floor in front of him. I tugged on his leash to make him come closer to me. He twisted and pulled at it in defiance. His hand squirted a liberal amount of the baby oil over his cock and balls.

"Where are my manners? You are all encouraged to help him. I don't care what you do to him. He will continue to stroke himself until he reaches that moment of truth. You will tease him and hurt him in whatever way you deem necessary," I disclosed.

They moved in for the kill with Emily kneeling behind him with her hands wrapped around his chest, manipulating his nipples with clothespins. Celeste grabbed his hair and pulled back hard enough to make him grimace.

Two others continually slapped his inflamed ass cheeks.

He was getting an overload of stimulus from a variety of sources. Hunter was begging me with his eyes to let him fire off. I shook my head to stave him from that pleasurable outlet.

I had told them that he would continue to stroke until he came. What they didn't know was that I was still in control. He had to wait in

excruciating agony for me to give him my nod of approval. Hunter fought that natural urge building until his balls had ballooned to twice their size.

The girls were laughing and having fun with my permission. They continued to call him every name in the book, including little piggy and cum slut. Their ridicule was the final straw that touched off a series of fireworks inside those bloated beach balls.

He screamed at the top of his lungs and took his hands away from his cock. It was angry and purple. I smiled and gave him my nod of

approval. He didn't have to touch it. Those erogenous zones on his

body were being stimulated, including a finger up his asshole.

His boiling jizz blew out of the end of his cock at my feet.

"I want you back here in one week." I emphasized the number one

with my finger raised so there would be no misunderstandings.

In one week, Chet, and the rest of them, were going to get the surprise of their lives.

<u>Chapter Twelve</u>
Esmerelda
One Week Later…

I'm having fun with the boys, but this may be taking things a little too far. Is there really such a thing? I don't need to know. I can't get enough of their humiliation and domination.

Brock was blindfolded with a ball gag in his mouth standing in the room when I entered with Chet in a similar position. They had no idea what was happening, but I suspected that they probably knew there was more than me in the room with them.

A pair of regulation police issued handcuffs were attached to Brock's wrists.

They were both naked, swinging in the breeze, waiting for the final shoe to drop. It came with me guiding Hunter by his elbow with his arms secured by a length of rope.

Chet had zip ties around his wrists and ankles.

They were separated by a six-foot distance on either side. I began by taking the blindfold off one after the other until their eyes adjusted to the glare of the fluorescent bulb swinging above them.

They were all mumbling in unison when they realized their friends were part of what I was up to. The ball gags came out, but I silenced their objections with a hand in the air.

"I don't see any reason to have your panties in a bunch. You're all under my control and what I say goes. Do I have to remind you about the punishment for disobedience?" I said, standing back to see my boys in their glory.

"At the risk of incurring your wrath, I would like to know what the hell is going on around here. Do you have any idea how awkward it is for us to be here together like this?" Hunter inquired, his cock quite pleased with this reversal of fortune.

"Don't stand there on some moral high ground. Your cock tells me that you like being watched by your friends." I pressed the remote control to bring his session to life on the screen.

He tried to look away, but it was like a car accident happening in slow motion.

Brock began laughing until I switched the screen for his session, taking it like a bitch on his hands and knees. I did the same thing with Chet. I laughed with evil intentions to see them squirm, unable to look each other in the eyes.

"Brock likes Elvis, but he positively adores Brutus," I announced with both lifelike dildos in my hands to show them the difference in size and thickness.

I brought it over to Brock and bent him over in front of his friends. One thrust of my hips buried Brutus deep, slick with a water-based lubricant. He howled with his entire body shaking. I had a firm hold of his hips for leverage to really make sure he received every inch.

I went at him for almost ten minutes with him screaming and moaning until I finally pulled out.

This time I replaced Brutus with Elvis and turned my attention to Chet's unused asshole. It was about time he learned the true meaning

of being dominated by a woman with something far larger than he possessed.

He was about to say something but stopped when I gave him a look to freeze the words in his throat.

"There's no reason to protest. You might want to say no, but your eyes say, fuck yes, let's do this. I would put the ball gag back in, but

I want to hear you take it like a man. It's not as big as Brutus. I don't want to hurt you the first time." I pressed on the small of his back to get him into the same position that Brock had been in.

I maneuvered us around until I could line up Hunter's cock with my wet, dirty little pussy, craving something to swallow. He was nothing more than a toy to be used for my amusement. I opened the zipper on the leather pants to give him easy access.

Feeling him throb when I grabbed the base and feeding him into the hot furnace of my love muffin was almost too much for me to take.

The real version was far more superior. The plastic version didn't compare.

I began rocking back and forth, feeding on the adrenaline rush of hearing Chet moan his compliance. I took my hands away from him and reached behind to attach vibrating nipple clamps to Hunter. His body went into spastic motions, which translated into a wild ride on the end of his cock.

"Damn, I didn't know that it could be this good fucking and getting fucked at the same time. Brock, crawl over here and put that mouth to work on my clit," I said, the words barely coming out of my mouth before he started toward me, crawling on all fours.

He looked a little timid about coming close to his friend's cock inside of me, but I could see he wasn't going to let me down. He didn't disappoint and showed a remarkable understanding of oral sex. It made me drive hard and relentlessly into Chet, almost forgetting about Hunter. He was the only one who hadn't been pegged, but I would rectify that miscarriage of justice.

Breathless and almost hitting that big O, I pulled out and stepped behind Hunter with both hands on his shoulders. He merely bent over when I signaled Brock to help feed Elvis into his asshole.

Brock was begging me with his eyes, but I wasn't paying attention.

Looking between my legs revealed that he had grabbed onto Elvis, still wet from being inside Chet's asshole.

"I give all of you straight A's for effort. I'm going to give each one of you ten strokes. Line up next to one another bent over, taking it like the bitches you are. I will give you the added incentive of cumming for me," I commanded, with each one performing to my expectations.

I went back and forth, taking my pleasure from their pain.

Slapping each ass in turn while I fucked them, one after the other. It was amazing in a way that I never thought possible. My nipples were hard and erect, and the wetness from my pussy dripped down my inner thigh.

"I want to fuck the cum out of each of you," I announced, Chet presently taking it until he was screaming, filling my hand with his warm load.

I brought it to his mouth, and he looked disgusted but proceeded to do as I requested until every drop was consumed.

I took my place behind Brock and fed his gaping hole with Brutus. He was the only one of the three that I was using that particular piece of rubber on. The other two were getting intimately acquainted with Elvis. Brock didn't make a sound except for a few whimpers until he bellowed his upcoming orgasm.

I captured it all in my hand, and he greedily lapped it up without a second thought.

"It looks like it's your turn." I snickered behind Hunter, grabbing onto his hips and giving it to him in one long deep stroke.

It took those final ten strokes to get him off. I was whispering each number into his ear, reminding him that he would only get one chance to blow his load.

I grunted, my legs fatigued from standing, thrusting my hips for almost an hour.

He came into my hand but was resistant to eat it. He was going to be a work in progress. The best I could accomplish was smearing it all over his face in a mask of white-hot cream. My fingers did slip into his mouth, covered in his cum.

I'm lucky that he didn't bite off my fingers in protest.

"I do believe there is one person in this room that hasn't been satisfied. I think you all know by now that one orgasm is never going to be enough for me. Take your positions on your hands and knees in front of me. It's not like you can use your hands, but your tongues are more than capable of helping me with this particular task."

It was their chance to choose where they were going to spend most of their time.

Chet seemed to be quite enamored with my leather boots and began feverishly licking and kissing them.

Brock projected an air of confidence when he stuck his tongue inside of me and began to flutter it in various rhythms. My legs quaked, and my inner thighs twitched uncontrollably. He was good and had no problem showing me how orally inclined he was.

Hunter moved in for the kill, his mouth latched onto my clit, stroking his tongue to make me weak at the knees.

"I've never had three guys going down on me. Chet, I want to feel your tongue beside Hunter's," I suggested.

He was hesitant. Still, he relented despite his better judgment.

The sloppy wet sounds of their mouths at work were like a symphony playing over and over again in my head. Light tremors began to grow with intensity until I was so close to orgasm that I had to stabilize myself on Chet's head.

The buildup was amazing, and I could feel a fire inside, ready to erupt. They must have sensed it because all three retreated to a safe distance, still on their knees with their mouths open.

I felt it coming, and I resisted until I couldn't stop even if I wanted to. My pussy sprayed everywhere, with no visible indication that it was going to slow down. It was the most explosive and wildly addictive orgasm of my life.

They watched me writhe as they drank from the fountain of my spewing orgasmic gush. It covered their faces and dripped down their naked bodies until I finally finished with a breathless whisper of thanks.

I held onto their heads and stroked their hair to signify that they had done an excellent job for their Mistress. They were in no hurry to get dressed, but I was through with them for the time being.

"I'm going to be seeing all of you regularly. Once a month, the three of you will come back at the same time to do this all over again. Let's see if we can improve on your performances. This is a gift, and I wouldn't squander it," I said to my captivated audience.

The boys turned and opened their hands to reveal their own personal cock cages and constricting cock rings.

They looked at me and at each other. I knew what they were thinking. They didn't want anything to do with other women.

"I expect you to wear them until my call comes for your next session. Now, get out of here. I'm tired of seeing your faces. Your Mistress needs to rest." I made a motion of my hand before releasing them from their bonds.

They closed the door behind them

Their stories have only just begun.

Wild Erotica From BJ Cuffs

Reader,

Thank you for taking the time to read Frat Boy Fun: Stories From the Dungeons Book 3. Make sure to snag your pre-order of Book 4, and keep up to date on all of my releases by joining my newsletter.

You never know where the whip will land next.

BJ

The Doc Is In: Stories From the Dungeons Book 4

Sneak Peek

Sneak Preview
The Doc Is In: Erotic Stories From The Dungeon Book 4

The stark white walls were clinical, lacking any personal touches. They were in desperate need of a splash of color here or there to bring life to the landscape.

Even his paintings were nothing more than bleak tabs of color, sparsely situated on random walls, shadows hiding the small stitch of vibrant hues.

The way Dr. Brantley arranged his desk, the perfect controlled lines, everything in its place, definitely signified that he was repressed sexually. The same thing could be said for many men, and women alike, when they weren't getting what they wanted at home.

My workers and I had a checklist, and it was our third day dealing with the doctor's constant complaints. Nothing was ever right in his *mistaken* opinion.

I was the recipient of the doc's tirades when he felt like lashing out at somebody.

Gail stood next to me as I worked away a smudge on the mirror in the patient bathroom, her voice barely a whisper. "I don't know what we're going to do with Sheila. I know she's the daughter of your friend, but she's not working out. I hate to be the bearer of bad news.

You must have noticed that her work ethic is simply atrocious. She's always on her phone talking to her boyfriend instead of working."

My cleaning business was a revolving door of employees. Gail had been with me for almost three months. That was unheard of in our line of work. Low pay and lack of benefits made my company a temporary landing spot for many.

"There's an adjustment period we have to account for. You're probably right. I'm just not willing to give up on her yet. Her mother is frantic that she's going down the wrong path. I want to give her another chance to prove herself. We all stumble and need a hand from time to time," I explained, watching Sheila over her shoulder filing her nails at the front desk.

Sheila was always malcontent, going against the grain to get under her mother's skin. The woman was crying out for help, and nobody could hear her. She was clinging to an older man that gave her that father figure she was missing in her life. It was a little weird for her to find that comfort in the arms of a mature man twice her age, but that wasn't my call.

"I don't see it getting any better. She doesn't want to be here anymore than we want her to be. It's taking twice as long to get things done with her on the squad. We gave her a simple assignment, to scrub out a coffee stain in the main examining room. She didn't even touch it," Gail pointed out, her head motioning toward the room down the hall.

The one thing I hate is people not doing what they're told. This doesn't happen in the dungeon...at least not very often.

It was the first I heard of the problem, and it was just few minutes before Dr. Brantley was going to walk through those doors to start his day.

Mondays were the worst. It only took a split second for him to zero in on a target and embellish the problem with wild gestures. His tone was not conducive to a good working relationship.

Learning his habits was one of my strengths. He was punctual to a fault. He expected the same adherence to the rules that he exercised himself every day. And he expected the women in his office to listen but not argue.

There was no denying his penchant for working his body into a temple. The fabric of his scrub pants stretched across his strong thighs, his shirt fell against the chiseled lines of his chest, and his short sleeves were rolled so tightly I imagined he busted a seam around his biceps on a regular basis. That physique made me want to make him my bitch. I could only wish for the day it would happen. If I didn't know better, I would have thought his gliding motions and pulse of muscles was for my viewing pleasure.

I hinted for Gail to leave as soon as possible with the rest of the squad, including Sheila. "I guess I'm going to have to take some action. That stain isn't going to clean itself. We both know how coffee stains can be quite formidable against any cleaner. It's horrible on carpets. It's a good thing I have a cleaning solution. It usually works on anything. There's not much time left. It was my idea to bring her on board. It seems only fitting that I should stick around to face the consequences."

"I don't know how I feel about leaving you to handle this. He doesn't take kindly to mistakes. We learned that the first day on the job. Her probation is getting on my last nerve. She doesn't know the meaning of hard work or the value of a dollar. I blame her mother for giving her everything she wanted on a silver platter."

I didn't like people trying to conform to conventional thinking. The exception was in the workplace, where rules are there for a reason. Rules worked even in my other life. It was best to put my foot down and show them it was my way or the highway from the very beginning. I couldn't be too hard on my employees, though. I had to keep them happy when all I could afford was minimum wage.

I pushed back the pieces of hair fluttering down on my sweat peppered brow and tugged at the waist of my coveralls. The dark blue uniform I wore was simply for professional appearances. Underneath, there was a guilty obsession hiding. Lace and satin rubbing softly against my skin.

I glanced over at Gail and sighed, nodding for the door. "We should give her until the end of the week. That way I can say that I tried and failed miserably. Her mother will see it as a lost cause and move on to something else. I have to give her the benefit of the doubt to see if she can change her ways under my direction. I'm going to have to get personally involved."

Gail flipped her blond hair behind her ears, her long curls touching the nape of her neck. "I know you're in a tough spot. It's not easy when friends call in a favor. I've been down that road a few times to know what I'm talking about. The two of us are older than the rest of the staff. We have to set an example. Don't let her get away with murder."

I admired Gail's straightforward approach. She would make the perfect protégé to pass on my expertise in a certain field of perversion. She could take that attitude and parlay it into more than ample compensation for her time. The only stumbling block was that I didn't like mixing business with pleasure.

Those two worlds had to remain separated. Some people could be very judgmental.

They packed up without Sheila lifting a finger to help. I shook my head at how easily the new generation could become complacent. They thought they had all the answers, but they didn't even know the questions. She was what I called a work in progress.

Giving up on her wasn't an option without exhausting every measure.

The team quickly left me alone in the office with less than five minutes left before the doctor was scheduled to walk through the doors. The stain was going to get me in trouble, but it was a good excuse to sneak a look at that perfect ass the doc carried around with him.

I knelt down on the floor and pulled my bag of cleaning supplies closer. The secret weapon to the coffee stain was in my bag of tricks. It was a recipe passed down from one generation to the other in my family. A lawyer was helping me to patent the process. It was a long exhausting path to take, but I felt it was worth it in the end.

The throw rug was woven and soft, the stain sunken all the way through the fabric. It probably would have been easier to throw it out, but the Doc would have noticed immediately that it was missing. The man had a keen eye for detail. It was one of the reasons why he was the most sought after gynecologists in the area.

His lack of a bedside manner didn't prevent the women from flocking to his office. He was the best in his field. And with that title came the cockiness. He was cocky about everything from his job to the way he treated women. Why he was so popular was beyond my understanding, except for maybe the way he would look diving down between my spread wide thighs.

I got down on my hands and knees in an unfamiliar position. Somebody was going to have to pay for this. I was resorting to manual labor. I was usually the supervisor, which hardly ever worked out due to my annoyingly nagging desire for perfection.

The sweetest release, though, came in the Dungeon.

The Dungeon is where I work out my issues. It's therapeutic.

All thoughts of my dark and damning abode fluttered away as I scrubbed the rug, my knuckles scraping on the fabric. The miracle cleaning solution was working, but it was going to take some time to lift that stain. It was time I didn't have with the ticking clock on the wall mocking me. It was painstaking work, and the effort made my arms burn.

I heard the telltale sound of a key in the lock down the hall. The very idea of the doctor standing over me in judgment gave me pause for thought.

The wreckage of his marriage was still a fresh wound. It was amazing what I could hear with my hearing aid. It wasn't as if I needed it. Nobody was aware that the handicap was a disguise to listen in on conversations. I became a fly on the wall.

A long deep sigh behind me froze my progress.

"This is the last time I'm going to say this. I hired your service for its discretion. You promised to be in and out without disturbing my normal morning routine. This is the second time I have found you in my office. I thought we had an understanding, but maybe we need to revisit the arrangement," Dr. Brantley addressed, wearing his crisp white lab coat with dark blue scrubs underneath.

"I only need another minute to get this stain out," I answered meekly, nothing like it was in the Dungeon.

"It's galling to think I'm paying good money for a service that hasn't lived up to my expectations. Is it too hard a concept for you to understand? I don't want to know you were here at all. I'm going to have to give this a lot of thought. This is very disappointing. Your assurances mean nothing to me. I don't want to hear excuses. I want to see results." He chastised me, his voice rising with each word.

It feels wrong to be subjected to his arrogant attitude. I don't like the taste of my own medicine. I wish there was some way to turn the tables. I'm just going to have to keep my eyes and ears open for a window of opportunity.

"Things like this happen and are usually unavoidable. I know what I promised. You don't have to remind me. The only thing I can do is apologize. Some things are out of my hands." I groveled to keep the contract, still on my hands and knees, looking up at him.

His hygiene was meticulous with gleaming white teeth. His dark hair was arranged perfectly without a single lock out of place, a peaking spray of salt and pepper threatening to come to life around his ears. His scrubs and jacket were pressed and clung tightly to his muscles. He believed in following the rules. Ironically, it was something we had in common in vastly different ways.

"This is unacceptable. You've already got two strikes against you. One more and I will have to look for another cleaning company. This will be the fourth one in the past six months. I thought yours would be different, but I should have known better to get my hopes up. My first patient will be here in five minutes. You better not be here when she…" He hesitated, the vein on his forehead throbbing in frustration.

His assistant Meredith was behind him, whispering into his ear about a potential problem.

He never even excused himself, walking away, dismissively, to handle the issue.

I resumed with my cleaning, scrubbing hard enough to make my fingers numb. I stopped and wiped gently back and forth and let out a sigh of relief. It was finally out without a moment to spare.

Tyrant...his wrath is fucking annoying. He thinks he's soooo important up there on his pathetic pedestal. Somebody needs to knock him back down to earth.

I used the waiting room seat to lift myself to a standing position. I was out of breath, completely exhausted. A good night's sleep with the drapes drawn during the day was my usual routine. This time, I would shake things up with a hot bath and soft music to lull my angry muscles into submission.

Glancing across the waiting room, I could see the Doc in a huff. He walked back and forth, pacing from the front door to the window without saying a word to his assistant.

I ducked back into his office before he had a chance to see me. Every time he turned, his eyes roved up and back down the perky young nurse. It felt dirty for me to stand there and witness the way that he was hungrily watching her.

I stood, my back against the wall, waiting for him to continue. It was just a matter of time before he stopped fuming internally and expressed himself with verbal commands of authority. She was brave under pressure and held her head high despite how he treated her like a second-class citizen.

Sheila could learn a thing or two about responsibility from her. That was another problem I would have to deal with at a later date. It was essential to give her the tools to set out independently without relying on mommy's money.

I'm beginning to think the answer is right in front of me. Why didn't I see it before?

Meredith and Sheila couldn't be less alike. They were night and day. Each one could teach the other something different.

"I don't want to hear it. This is your blunder. I pay you good money to handle these problems without bothering me. Don't make me regret hiring you. I have a simple set of standards that I require everybody to follow religiously," he argued.

"I will call and reschedule your 10:00 appointment. She's not going to be very happy," Meredith stated, her voice lowered to prevent any possibility of incurring his wrath.

I knew enough to know that her loyalty was without question. She was not immune to the harsh way he spoke to her, but somehow, she stood her ground. Never once did I hear her say that it was his fault. She would always find the right words without making any snap judgments.

The woman is a paragon of virtue. I just wish that he valued her in the way that she deserves.

My hearing aid was picking up something in the background. It was coming from his phone. It was left carelessly on his desk. My curiosity got the best of me, and I turned my attention to the screen. Slowly, a grin pulled over my lips.

I turned up the volume. "I see that somebody is running a fever. I have just the thing for that. Let me lift my uniform and show you where I'm going to take your temperature," the seductive female voice directed.

It appeared my strait-laced employer had a secret fetish. It revolved around being with a nurse. Now that was something I could work with.

I reached into the pocket of my scratchy blue overalls and carefully pulled out my black card with shimmering gold lettering. Nonchalantly, I pressed it to my palm and slid my hand across the slick mahogany desktop, leaving the card inconspicuously behind. It was just peeking out of the first file folder of the day.

It was going to be interesting to see what his sexual appetite revealed. His divorce was causing him nothing but problems, even if it was all self-induced from anxiety and stress. I could be the solution if he was willing to open himself to the possibilities. It stood to reason he would be hesitant, but the little voice in the head between his legs would convince him to take a chance.

I can hardly wait to get my hands on him. This won't be just for me. This will be for all the girls he has ogled and those who have felt his demeaning words. A lesson is going to be learned the hard way. I have just the outfit. It's not often I get the chance to role-play nurse.

I walked out of there without saying another word to him. I could almost feel his glaring eyes of disapproval boring a hole through my skull but it made no difference to me.

He's the type of man that will have to sleep on it for a night. He has no idea what he's about to walk into, but he's not gonna know what hit him when he does. The Doctor is in, but the Nurse is gonna run this show.